UNICORNS

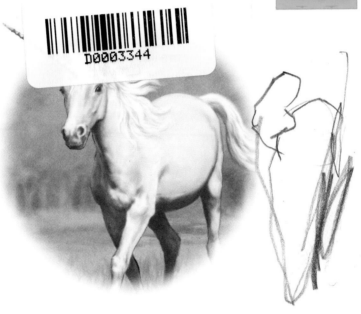

by Lucille Recht Penner
illustrated by Mel Grant

A STEPPING STONE BOOK™

Random House 🏠 New York

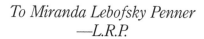

To Miranda Lebofsky Penner
—L.R.P.

To Lynn and Julie—and, of course, Curious-Jen . . .
whom I dare not leave out—and all those young
dreamers who would ride a unicorn
—M.G.

Text copyright © 2005 by Lucille Recht Penner. Illustrations copyright © 2005 by Mel Grant. All rights reserved under International and Pan-American Copyright Conventions. Published in the United States by Random House Children's Books, a division of Random House, Inc., New York, and simultaneously in Canada by Random House of Canada Limited, Toronto.

www.steppingstonesbooks.com
www.randomhouse.com/kids
www.melgrant.com

Library of Congress Cataloging-in-Publication Data
Penner, Lucille Recht.
Unicorns / by Lucille Recht Penner ; illustrated by Mel Grant. — 1st ed.
    p.   cm.
"A Stepping Stone Book."
ISBN 0-375-83008-1 (pbk.) — ISBN 0-375-93008-6 (lib. bdg.)
1. Unicorns.   I. Grant, Mel, ill.   II. Title.
GR830.U6P46 2005   398'.469—dc22   2005000853

First Edition
Printed in the United States of America   10 9 8 7 6 5 4 3 2 1

RANDOM HOUSE and colophon are registered trademarks and A STEPPING STONE BOOK and colophon are trademarks of Random House, Inc.

Contents

1
The Unicorn Myth

The sun goes down. It is dark in the forest. A deep pond glitters in the moonlight.

One by one, thirsty animals gather around the pond. But they are afraid to drink. They know that snakes drink from the pond during the day. The snakes poison the water.

The animals wait. A gentle breeze blows

toward them. *They sniff the air. Help is coming!*

A graceful white shape glides silently out of the trees. It is a unicorn. The unicorn kneels down and dips its long silver horn into the pool. Then it rises and bounds away.

The animals lower their heads and drink. The unicorn's horn is magical. It has made the water safe.

This story about a unicorn is hundreds of years old. There are many, many old stories about unicorns.

In some stories, unicorns are huge and fierce. In others, they are small and gentle.

Most are shy and live alone. A few are playful. They like to run and leap with other unicorns.

In one way, though, all unicorns are the same. Each one has a single horn in the middle of its forehead. *Unicorn* means "one horn."

Why are there so many stories about unicorns?

Some people thought they had seen them.

A beautiful antelope called an oryx lives in Africa. An oryx has two horns. But if you see it from the side, one horn is hidden

behind the other. It looks as if the oryx has only one horn. The early Egyptians painted pictures of the oryx that looked that way . . . like a unicorn!

Maybe this is one way legends about unicorns began. A person saw the pictures. He told another person. Parents told their children. And over the years, people grew up believing in unicorns.

2
The European Unicorn

People around the world imagined unicorns in different ways. A European unicorn was enchanting. It was white as snow with a soft, flowing mane and silky tail. A spiral horn grew out of its forehead. The horn was made of ivory, but it gleamed like silver in the moonlight and sparkled like gold in the sun.

From a distance, it was possible to mistake a European unicorn for a horse. They were about the same size. But unicorns ran faster than horses. And farther. They could run for a hundred miles without getting tired. Nobody riding a horse could catch one.

A sweet smell of cinnamon was often the only way to tell if this kind of unicorn was nearby. Hardly anybody ever saw one because they were very shy. They spent most of their time hidden away far from people. Their favorite places were deep forests where tall trees grew close together.

Male unicorns lived by themselves. Babies lived with their mothers, who kept them hidden in the darkest part of the forest. Sometimes mother unicorns met in a field of flowers and let their babies play together.

Then they hurried back into the forest.

A baby unicorn could not protect itself. It was born without a horn. But its horn started to grow right away. It took about a year for a baby unicorn to grow to its full size. Then it went off to live by itself in the woods.

You have probably seen pictures of European unicorns. Artists have been painting them for hundreds of years. But there were also many other kinds of unicorns roaming the world.

3
The *Ki-lin* and the *Kirin*

The Chinese unicorn is called the *ki-lin* (KEE-lin). It was a beautiful animal, but strange-looking.

It had scales like a dragon. It had a beard and a long mane and tail. Its coat was a rainbow of bright colors—red, blue, yellow, black, and white. Its long horn was made of pure silver.

Ki-lins were kind. *Ki-lins* would never fight with other animals. They never even stepped on an ant. In fact, a soft piece of skin grew over the tip of their horns so that they could never harm anyone, even by mistake.

The great emperor Fu Hsi stared into the Yellow River. A ki-lin *splashed out of the water. The emperor was amazed! The* ki-lin *knelt down in front of the emperor. On its back was a scroll. The emperor spread out the scroll and saw a map of his kingdom. Strange marks were drawn next to the rivers and towns.*

The emperor stared at the marks for a

long time. Finally he figured out that they were writing. The ki-lin *had given him a written language. Now his people would be able to write down and remember everything that happened to them.*

Whenever a *ki-lin* was seen, something wonderful happened. They were often seen before the birth of a great man. If an emperor saw one, the next years would be happy ones for him and his people.

A pregnant woman was walking in the forest. A ki-lin *came up to her. She stroked its head. It gave her a beautiful piece of green jade.*

Soon the woman lay down and fell

asleep. When she woke up, the ki-lin *was* gone. Was it a dream? No, the jade was still in her hand. It had words carved on it.

The words said that she would give birth to a son who would be an important man. When her baby was born, the woman named him Confucius (kun-FEW-shus). He became a great teacher.

In ancient times, Chinese women hoped to see a *ki-lin* before their babies were born. They drew pictures of the god of childbirth riding on a *ki-lin*. They hung the pictures on the walls of their houses.

The *kirin* (KEE-rin) was a Japanese unicorn. *Kirins* were many sizes. Some were as small as goats. Others were as big as bulls. A few looked like lions. They were gold in color and had thick manes and big paws.

All *kirins* had bristly eyebrows and fierce eyes. People who looked into the eyes of a *kirin* sometimes became so scared that they couldn't move at all. They felt as if they had been turned to stone.

A *kirin* had a special power. It could tell good from evil. Long ago, Japanese judges let a *kirin* decide if a person was guilty of a crime.

The *kirin* was brought into the courtroom. It stared at the person on trial. If the *kirin* decided the person was guilty, it stabbed him through the heart with its horn.

Kirins were scary. But another kind of unicorn was even more frightening!

4
The *Karkadann*

In Arabia and Persia long ago, there were lots of wild animals to watch out for. Wolves. Tigers. Snakes. But the most scary animal was a unicorn called a *karkadann* (KAR-kuh-dan).

What did a *karkadann* look like? It was as big as a rhinoceros. It had three hooves on each leg and the tail of a lion. When it bellowed, other animals ran away. Birds flew into treetops.

A *karkadann* would fight anything. Most animals would hide when they saw it coming.

Could anybody tame a *karkadann*?

Philip was a famous king. One of his subjects gave him a wild baby karkadann. *His soldiers tried to ride it. The* karkadann *threw them all off.*

Alexander, Philip's son, asked if he could try. The soldiers laughed because the boy was only thirteen. They began making bets. Could Alexander stay on the karkadann?

King Philip said to go ahead. Alexander

walked up to the karkadann. *He spoke to it softly. He patted its mane.*

The karkadann *let him climb on its back. They rode off. Everyone cheered. King Philip was proud. He gave the* karkadann *to his son.*

The boy in this story grew up to be Alexander the Great, a mighty warrior. His unicorn grew up, too. It became big and fierce. Alexander always rode it into battle. Together they won many lands.

Alexander's enemies were jealous. They thought his *karkadann* helped him win. They all wanted one. But nothing was harder than catching a unicorn.

5
How to Capture
a Unicorn

People were always trying to capture unicorns. Most were caught when they were young and small. Alexander tamed his *karkadann* when it was still a baby.

If a unicorn was attacked, it fought back. A unicorn was a good fighter. It was smart and quick. It ran faster than the fastest horses and hunting dogs.

Sometimes hunters could trap a unicorn if a young girl helped them.

The huntsmen and their dogs wait in a garden filled with flowers. They see a unicorn. The hunters blow their trumpets and gallop toward it. The unicorn kicks out. It swings its horn to defend itself.

It gets away. But it sees a girl in the woods. The unicorn stops and puts its head in her lap. She strokes it gently.

The hunters ride up. They capture the unicorn and put it in a pretty fenced garden.

This story is shown in a set of seven tapestries. They were woven over five hundred years ago. They hung in a house

in France. In the 1700s, peasants broke into the house. They took the tapestries. They used them to protect fruit trees from frost and to cover potatoes in their barns.

Many years later, the owners got the tapestries back. Today they hang in a museum in New York City. Thousands of people see them every year.

The story that the tapestries tell seems strange. Why would anyone want to hunt a unicorn?

The answer is that people wanted unicorn horns. They believed that these horns had strange and magical powers.

6
Unicorn Magic

In the Middle Ages, people worried a lot about poison. It was an easy way for someone to hurt his enemies. How could a person tell if his food was poisoned?

The best way was with a unicorn horn. When poison was nearby, the horn started to sweat. At meals, rich people would put a unicorn horn in the middle of the table. If a person couldn't afford a whole horn, he used a little piece of one.

Doctors made unicorn-horn medicine. They scraped tiny bits off a horn and mixed them with water. Then they gave the mixture to a sick person to drink. This was a powerful cure for many sicknesses. In fact, if a few grains of horn were put on a person's tongue right after he died, it sometimes brought him back to life!

Unicorn horns cost a lot of money. Some people tried to sell fake ones. But there were ways to tell if a unicorn horn was real. If you dropped a piece of it into water, it sent up bubbles. If you burned a piece, it made a sweet scent. But the best test was to try it out with poison.

A king paid a fortune for a unicorn horn. To make sure it was real, he dipped it in poisoned water. Then he told one of his servants to drink the water.

The servant drank it and died right away. The king was angry! He had been sold a fake unicorn horn!

A unicorn horn could do more than check for poison and cure diseases. It helped people's memory. It even kept them young. So of course everyone wanted one. And in the 1200s, sailors began bringing horns to Europe from faraway places.

The horns were real. But did they come from real unicorns?

7
Sea Unicorns?

A long time ago, people believed that
for every animal that lived on land a similar
animal lived in the sea. Horses, for example,
lived on land and sea horses lived in the
sea.

What about unicorns? In the Middle
Ages, people began hearing reports of a
sea unicorn. Hardly anybody had seen one.

Sea unicorns lived in the freezing ocean near the North Pole. They died if they were taken away from their home.

The sea unicorn is actually a kind of whale called a narwhal (NAR-wall).

Narwhals are huge. They have eight-foot-long horns sticking out of their heads. The horns are pure ivory and grow in a spiral—just like a unicorn horn!

But are narwhals really sea unicorns? Sailors thought they knew how to find out.

First they cut off a horn. It was hollow inside. They put poisonous spiders into it and sealed it shut.

When they opened it, the spiders were

dead. They had died from lack of air. But
the sailors didn't know that. They thought
the horn had killed the spiders because
they were poisonous. So the sea unicorn
must be real!

Still, a sea unicorn wasn't the same as a land unicorn. And people who had paid a fortune for *real* unicorn horns began to worry. What if their horns came from sea unicorns? What if sea unicorn horns didn't have the same magical powers?

And then they began to wonder. Were land unicorn horns fake, too?

As the years went by, scientists stopped believing in unicorns. Doctors stopped using unicorn-horn medicine. Hardly anyone went searching for unicorns.

8
A Living Unicorn

"Come see the living unicorn!"

In the 1980s, the Ringling Bros. and Barnum & Bailey circus showed off a new animal to the world. A living unicorn! It was pure white, with a long, fluffy mane and tail. A single horn stuck out of its forehead.

Everyone who saw it was thrilled.

Except for one little girl. She said, "It looks like a goat." And that's what it was.

A couple that lived in California had
made it from a baby Angora goat. They
never told anyone how they did it. But it
wasn't the first time it had been done.
People had "made" unicorns before.

Thousands of years ago, Roman farmers twisted the soft horns of young rams together. The horns joined together and became one horn.

In Sudan, Dinka tribesmen operated on large baby bulls so that they had only one horn. They trained the one-horned bulls to be the leaders of their herds.

Why would anyone do that?

Just as in the legends, an animal with one horn is a good fighter. Other animals run away when they see a sharp horn pointed at them. If a one-horned bull has to fight, it can put all its weight behind its horn. Animals with two horns have to turn their heads from side to side to fight.

In 1933, Dr. W. Franklin Dove decided to make a unicorn bull. He picked a male calf that was one day old. Dr. Dove knew that horns grow from tissue on each side of a calf's skull. These bits of tissue are called "horn buds."

Dr. Dove moved the horn buds to the front of the calf's skull above its eyes. He put the two buds right next to each other. Then he waited and watched. As the calf grew, the buds joined into one horn.

Dr. Dove's bull was the strongest animal in the herd. It was also the gentlest. Just like a unicorn in stories and myths.

Some people get angry about these
kinds of unicorns. They think it is mean to
the goats, rams, and bulls. And they say
these animals are not *real* unicorns.

Other people wonder whether real unicorns are still living in faraway places. Do they exist today? Did these fabulous creatures ever exist?

What do *you* think?